# You Can Be
# Santa's Helper

GEORGE COMEAUX

*George Comeaux*       *Mary T. Bodio*

## You Can Be Santa's Helper

ISBN: 1-4392-1109-4
ISBN-13: 9781439211090
Library of Congress Control Number: 2008908482

**Visit www.booksurge.com to order additional copies.**

or please contact us at BookSurge Publishing
1-866-308-6235

**orders@booksurge.com**

*Printed in North Charleston, S.C.
U.S.A.*

*To Caitlyn from Santa*

## DEDICATION

**For Santa's Helpers everywhere,**
especially…

**For my parents and siblings,**
for sharing the spirit of Christmas as Santa's Helpers to each other

**and**

**For my family,**
for continuing the tradition

**and**

**For the staff and volunteers at My Brother's Keeper**
www.mybrotherskeeper.org
an organization of Santa's Helpers in North Easton, Massachusetts, which delivers food and furniture to those in need throughout the year, and turns its warehouse into Santa's Workshop at Thanksgiving, delivering "the love and hope of Christ" to hundreds of local families (and for similar organizations everywhere)

**and**

**For Stella,**
Mary Bodio's granddaughter,
the model Santa's Helper in this book

**and**

**For YOU!**
## You can be Santa's Helper!

# ACKNOWLEDGMENTS

Several very special people influenced this publication:

My sister Carolyn suggested that "You Can Be Santa's Helper" should be published as a Christmas book.

My brother Mike wrote the music, and the song was first performed by the "On a Wing and a Prayer" ensemble of Immaculate Conception Parish in North Easton, Massachusetts, as part of a fund-raising variety show, "Holi-daze."

My parents established the basis for the lyric, the "Santa's Helper" routine with which we celebrated each Christmas. I was the second child of a family that expanded to thirteen children. In the early days, Mom and Dad would announce a "ten dollar limit," and we siblings would draw names for one additional gift exchange. Individually, some might say there was a shortage. Collectively, there was a surplus. The youngest family member (at the time) selected a gift from under the tree, exclaimed "Ho! Ho! Ho!," and presented the gift to its recipient, and the rotation proceeded up through the ages, including adults. The only rules were, don't choose a gift for yourself, and no two gifts in a row for the same person. Thus, each family member participated in each gift.

(Occasionally, there might be a lapse in Christmas spirit. I have apologized to my younger sister Chris for this lapse. One Christmas, she drew my name. When I opened her gift, I blurted, "It's a handkerchief, only ten cents!" Now I confess publicly – fifty years later, the handkerchief she carefully personalized by embroidering my initial is the only exchange gift I remember!)

My late wife Maureen and our seven children continued the tradition. With our children grown and dispersed, a few years ago Dan and Jill and their three children were my only Christmas visitors. I suggested we should race through opening the gifts on Christmas Eve. Dan said "No Way!", and restored my spirit. I am still Santa's Helper every Christmas!

Additionally, my friend Maureen Yachimski supported the process of putting this book together, with extensive patience, proofreading, and consultation on the final publication decisions for *You Can Be Santa's Helper.*

Santa Claus has lots to do
At the North Pole, all year through.
Who will help him? Why not you?
You can be his helper, too!

Here we are
Here we go —

Ha Ha Ha! Ho Ho Ho!
Here we are, here we go!
Here we are, here we go!
Ha Ha Ha Ha! — Ho Ho Ho!

You can be Santa's helper
Every Christmas, and all year —
Help him change tears to laughter!
Help him spread joy and cheer!

Ha Ha Ha! Ho Ho Ho!
Here we are, here we go!
Here we are, here we go!
Ha Ha Ha Ha! — Ho Ho Ho!

Santa isn't rich and handsome,
And it's true, he weighs a ton.
Santa doesn't make a million,
But he's always number one!

'Cause he travels all the world,
From beginning to the end,
Finding everyone who's lonely,
Making everyone his friend!

Ha Ha Ha! Ho Ho Ho!
Here we are, here we go!
Here we are, here we go!
Ha Ha Ha Ha! — Ho Ho Ho!

Santa travels all alone,
With his reindeer in his sleigh,

And the love he leaves at your house
Is for you to give away!

Ha Ha Ha! Ho Ho Ho!
Here we are, here we go!
Here we are, here we go!
Ha Ha Ha Ha! — Ho Ho Ho!

Help your friend, and your neighbor,
And don't wait for their applause.
When you help someone who needs you,
You're helping Santa Claus!

Ha Ha Ha! Ho Ho Ho!
Here we are, here we go!
Here we are, here we go!
Ha Ha Ha Ha! — Ho Ho Ho!

Help your brother, and your sister,
And don't wait for their applause.
Help your Mother and your Father,
And you're helping Santa Claus!

You can be Santa's helper
Every Christmas, and all year —
Help him change tears to laughter!
Help him spread joy and cheer!

And if some year, Christmas Eve,
Santa Claus gets very sick —
You may get a call from Santa —
"Ride with Rudolph — Be Saint Nick!"

You can be Santa's helper
Every Christmas, and all year —
Help him change tears to laughter!
Help him spread joy and cheer!

Ha Ha Ha! Ho Ho Ho!
Here we are, here we go!
Here we are, here we go!
Ha Ha Ha Ha! — Ho Ho Ho!

# You Can Be Santa's Helper

George E. Comeaux

Words/Music Copyright 2008 G.E. Comeaux/J.M. Comeaux

# You Can Be Santa's Helper

San - ta is - n't rich and hand - some, and it's true, he weighs a

ton! San - ta does - n't make a mil - lion, but he's al - ways num - ber

one! _____ 'Cause he

tra - vels all the world, from be - gin - ning, to the end, fin - ding

ev - 'ry one who's lone - ly, ma - king ev - 'ry one his

friend! _____

Ha Ha Ha! Ho Ho Ho! Here we are and here we go!

Here we are! Here we go! Ha Ha Ha Ha! Ho Ho Ho!

Help your

bro - ther and ___ your sis - ter, and don't wait for their ap - plause ___ Help your

mo - ther and your fa - ther, and you're help - ing San - ta Claus! ___ You can

be San - ta's ___ Hel - per, ev - 'ry Christ - mas, and all year! ___ Help him

And if, some year, Christ mas Eve, San - ta Claus gets ve - ry

sick, You may get a call from San - ta, "Ride with Ru - dolph, be St.

Nick!" You can be San - ta's

Hel - per_____ ev-'ry Christ - mas, and all year!___ Help him

change tears_ to laugh - ter, help him spread joy... ... and

cheer! _____

Ha Ha Ha! Ho Ho Ho! Here we are and here we go!

Here we are! Here we go! Ha Ha Ha Ha! Ho Ho Ho!

Here we are, and a here we go! Ha Ha Ha Ha! Ho Ho Ho!

Made in the USA